Tim O'Toole and the Wee Folk

An Irish Tale Told and Illustrated by
GERALD McDERMOTT

PUFFIN BOOKS

PUFFIN BOOKS
Published by the Penguin Group
Viking Penguin, a division of Penguin Books USA Inc.,
375 Hudson Street, New York, New York 10014, U.S.A.
Penguin Books Ltd, 27 Wrights Lane, London W8 5TZ, England
Penguin Books Australia Ltd, Ringwood, Victoria, Australia
Penguin Books Canada Ltd, 10 Alcorn Avenue, Toronto, Ontario, Canada M4V 3B2
Penguin Books (N.Z.) Ltd, 182–190 Wairau Road, Auckland 10, New Zealand

Penguin Books Ltd, Registered Offices: Harmondsworth, Middlesex, England

First published in the United States of America by Viking Penguin, a division
of Penguin Books USA Inc., 1990
Published in Puffin Books, 1992
1 3 5 7 9 10 8 6 4 2
Copyright © Gerald McDermott, 1990
All rights reserved

LIBRARY OF CONGRESS CATALOGING-IN-PUBLICATION DATA
McDermott, Gerald.
Tim O'Toole and the wee folk / by Gerald McDermott.   p. cm.
Summary: A very poor Irishman is provided with magical things by
the "wee folk," but he must then keep his good fortune out of the
hands of the greedy McGoons.
ISBN 0-14-050675-6
[1. Fairy tales.   2. Ireland—Fiction.]   I. Title.
[PZ8.M4576 Ti 1992]   [E]—dc20   91-31469

Printed in the United States of America
Set in Sabon

In a little cottage, on a little hill, at the end of a little lane in Donegal, lived Tim O'Toole and his wife, Kathleen. Tim and Kate were so poor they had not a penny or a potato between them. Their children ate porridge for supper. Even the mice were thin from want of food and the cat wouldn't bother with chasing the creatures.

Their neighbors, who were poor enough themselves, avoided Tim, for they thought he would bring them bad luck. Things went from bad to worse until one day there was not a crumb or a drop left in the house.

"Tim O'Toole," said Kate. "I can stand no more of being poor, and you sitting around bemoaning your fate. You must go out to find work like a decent man and take us out of this poverty."

Kathleen kept after him, and next morning Tim set out to see if he could earn some wages.

Tim O'Toole traveled the length of the county, knocking at every door, inquiring at every farm, trying to eke out a few coppers for a day's work. But there was no work to be had. Finally, when Tim was tired and hungry and could walk no further, he stopped and lay down to rest in the cool, green clover at the side of the road.

No sooner had he stretched out then he heard the faint sound of merry piping and lilting voices raised in song and laughter. The strange music was coming from a little hollow in the side of the hill.

Tim crept up to the hollow and peered over the edge.
There below him was a troop of the wee folk, laughing
and singing and carrying on. Well, Tim knew for sure his
luck had changed, for it is well known that whoever
spies the wee folk in the light of day can
demand their treasure.

Suddenly, the music stopped. The little merrymakers were astonished when they looked up and saw Tim peering down at them.

"Hand over your gold!" bellowed Tim, trying to be fierce, "and you'll come to no harm."

"Have mercy on us, Tim O'Toole," begged the leader of the little people. There was a smile on his lips and he tried not to laugh. "You've caught us for fair so we'll see that you're richly rewarded."

Then there was hurrying and scurrying in the hollow below and soon the wee folk handed up a little gray goose.

"Here you are, Tim. A goose that lays golden eggs. Go home straightaway, tell not a soul, and you and your Kate shall never want for more."

Tim started for home, carrying the goose and feeling very pleased with himself. Soon darkness overcame him and he stopped at a farmhouse to ask if he could stay the night. The couple who owned the farm, the McGoons, let him in and sat him down by the fire. Tim began to boast of his great good fortune and the little gray goose that lays golden eggs.

That night, while Tim was asleep in the loft, the McGoons decided they could use just such a goose as this. Quietly, they exchanged it for their own.

Tim was none the wiser for it and in the morning went happily homeward, carrying the goose he thought would bring him great wealth. When he got home, he put the bird upon the table.

"Is this all you've to show for being gone these three days?" asked Kathleen.

"But darlin', this is no ordinary goose," said Tim. "This one lays golden eggs!"

Well, the short of it is, they waited a long, long time and, as you might guess, the goose did no such thing. "They've cheated me!" howled Tim, and he marched off in a terrible temper to give the little people what for. When he finally reached their hiding place, he was still angry.

"Golden eggs, is it?" cried Tim to the wee folk. "That goose you gave me laid no eggs at all!"

"This is curious, indeed," said their startled leader. Then the little man wrinkled his nose and gave a sly smile. "Tim, wait but a moment and we'll make good your reward.

There was hurrying and scurrying in the hollow below. A moment later, the wee folk brought forth a fine linen tablecloth and spread it in front of Tim. In the wink of an eye, it was covered with bounteous food and drink the likes of which he had never seen before.

"Take this tablecloth home straightaway, Tim O'Toole, and tell not a soul," cautioned the leader of the little ones. "Then you and your darlin' Kate shall never want for more."

Tim walked merrily toward home until darkness came on him. Again he stayed the night with the McGoons, and boasted to them of his newfound fortune. The McGoons thought it good fortune indeed. While Tim slept, they slipped away the magic tablecloth and exchanged it for an ordinary one from their very own cupboard.

Tim was none the wiser for it when he reached home the next day.

"Kathleen, my darlin'," he said. "We'll never go hungry again."

With a flourish, he spread the cloth upon the table. Well, of course, it was empty and produced not a drop or a crumb.

Kathleen laughed. Tim went into a rage.

"The little heathens!" he shouted.

In a flash, Tim was out the door and on the road again.

"Stand fast!" Tim called down into the little hollow where the wee folk were gathered.

"'Tis pleased you are not, Tim O'Toole," said the leader. "Could it be that the tablecloth was empty?" All the wee folk were grinning.

"Indeed it was, you scoundrel!" answered Tim.

The wee ones began to chuckle.

"And did you go direct home, as we told you?"

Tim O'Toole admitted he had twice stayed the night at the McGoons. When they heard this, the little people burst into laughter.

"You were a fool to trust the likes of the McGoons," said the leader. "But never mind, Tim. We've just the thing for you."

The little people brought up a strange green hat and gave it to Tim. They instructed him to boast of its magic to the McGoons, and to leave the hat where they could find it.

"Then we shall see what we shall see," said the wee one.

A third time, Tim tarried at the McGoons.
He proudly displayed the magic hat the wee
folk had given him. Then he crawled up into
the loft and pretended to sleep. He had but laid
his head upon the straw when he heard the
McGoons stir below.

"I wonder what sort of magic it is?" said
McGoon to his wife.

Cautiously, he tipped over the hat.

Out of the hat jumped ten tiny men. Each had a little blackthorn club and began to beat the McGoons about the shins and ankles. The couple whooped and hollered and danced around the room, trying to escape the blows of the wee folk. "Lay off! Lay off!" begged McGoon. "Tell your henchmen to have mercy, O'Toole."

"Give me my linen tablecloth and my little gray goose and I'll leave you in peace," said Tim, laughing all the while.

The McGoons gave back what they had taken. Tim put on his hat, tucked the little gray goose under one arm, draped the tablecloth over the other arm, and headed for home.

When Tim arrived, he spread the tablecloth before Kathleen and set down the goose in the middle of it. The bird honked and laid a golden egg. Then the most delectable eatables and drinkables began magically to appear on the table.

"Kathleen, my darlin'," said Tim. "We are happy at last."

Or so Tim thought.

Folks from all parts soon heard of the O'Toole's good fortune and crowded in to see the wondrous goose. Their little cottage filled up with neighbors until there was no place left to sit or to stand. Everyone helped themselves to the never-ending supply of eatables and drinkables. "I never knew we had so many friends," said Tim. "But I think 'tis time the party was at an end." Tim tipped his hat and out jumped the ten tiny men with blackthorn clubs. They beat the shins and ankles of the noisy crowd, chased them out of the house, and pursued them down the hill.

After that, the cottage was quiet once again. Tim O'Toole and his family were quite comfortable, you might say. They spent many hours in front of the hearth, sipping hot tea, and chatting, and thinking kind thoughts of the wee folk.

For all I know, Tim and Kate are there still, in a little cottage, on a little hill, at the end of a little lane in Donegal.